For Freddie and Bianca

Library of Congress Cataloging-in-Publication Data

D'Amico, Carmela.

Ella takes the cake / by Carmela D'Amico ; illustrated by Steven D'Amico.– 1st ed.   p. cm.

Summary: Ella the elephant wants to help in her mother's bakery,

but will the job she takes on prove to be more than she can handle?

ISBN 0-439-62794-X

[1. Elephants—Fiction. 2. Bakers and bakeries—Fiction.] I. D'Amico, Steven, ill. II. Title.

PZ7.D1837Elh 2005   [E]—dc22   2004023432

10 9 8 7 6 5 4 3 2 1   05 06 07 08 09

First edition, September 2005   Printed in Singapore   46

Book design by Steven D'Amico and David Saylor

The text was set in 20-point Aged.

ella
takes the cake

by carmela & steven d'amico

ARTHUR A. LEVINE BOOKS

An Imprint of Scholastic Inc.

Ella and her mother had lived
in Little Village for nearly a year.

It was already summer vacation and the bakery was busier than ever. Ella tried her best to help.

But sometimes, she didn't feel very helpful.
She'd already swept the floor three times.
There wasn't a crumb on it.

When the oven timer went off — *DING!* — Ella thought she'd help by taking out the macaroons.

"No, no, no," her mother sang. "You might burn yourself."

"I'd like a piece of the pineapple pie," said the next lady in line.

"I'll cut you a slice," offered Ella.

"No," her mother said. "I will. The pie knife's very sharp."

"But I want to help," said Ella.

"You *are* helping," her mother replied.

When Mr. Banjo came to pick up the day's deliveries, the bakery was still very busy.

Ella's mother rushed outside
and called to him, but he didn't hear.
"What's the matter?" Ella asked.
"Oh, Mr. Banjo's forgotten a cake again," she sighed. "And this one was supposed to be at the lighthouse by noon."

Ella wished she could help. But what could she do? She thought and she thought. Then she said, "I have an idea!"

"Well, Ella," her mother laughed, "this will be *very* helpful. But please be careful. Go directly to Captain Kernel's lighthouse."

"Don't worry," Ella said happily. "I promise I will."

She eagerly pedaled off, but her
mother called out after her: "Ella!
Ella! Don't forget your lucky hat!"

As Ella passed the fire station, she spotted Belinda sitting on the curb.

"Hey!" shouted Belinda. "Can I have a ride?"

"But there's not enough room," protested Ella.

"Sure there is. I'll make room," said Belinda, squeezing in.

In the marketplace, they passed Miss Melba.

"Ella! Belinda! Where are you going?"

"We're on our way to the lighthouse to deliver this cake," Ella said. "How about you?"

"I'm on my way to the hospital to deliver these fresh bananas."

"Well, we're headed that way," Ella said. "We'd be glad to take them for you."

Miss Melba beamed at her. "You are so sweet, Ella! But it's such a beautiful day, I look forward to the walk."

Around the next corner, they ran into Mr. Sneed.
"Hey, Mr. Sneed!" Belinda said. "Where are
you taking those books? Because I could take
them for you, if you want. I'd be glad to!"

"I'm taking them to the library.
But are you sure you have enough room?"
"Sure I'm sure!" said Belinda.

The library was *not* on the way. And books are heavy! But Mr. Sneed looked so relieved that Ella couldn't object.

"Next stop, the library," she said.
"But the library's *so boooring*," groaned Belinda.
"Hey, I have an idea! Let's go to the Village Square!"

"We can't," Ella said. "We have deliveries to make!"

"All right." Belinda shrugged. "I guess I'll go alone."

"But I was going to ask you to push!" said Ella.

"Well," asked Belinda, "what would you have done without me?"

Without Belinda to help her, Ella had to pedal with all her might.

Finally, she reached the library.
Wobbling off her bicycle, Ella unlatched the back of the wagon.

But the hill was just a bit too . . .

. . . steep.

The cake started to slide out too . . .

. . . though Ella managed to stop it just in time.
"Thank goodness!" she gasped with relief.

It was much later than Ella had thought!
How could she carry all those books into
the library quickly? She grabbed her lucky hat.

Much to her surprise, no matter how many books she put inside, there was always room for another.

Ella dashed from the library just in time to see the cart break loose . . .

SNAP!

. . . and go barreling down the hill!

She raced after the cake . . .

. . . past the marketplace . . .

. . . through the Square . . .

. . . and toward the water!

Fortunately, the drawbridge operator had seen them coming.

Clickety, clickety, click: He lifted the drawbridge up quickly!

Back on her way, Ella crossed paths with Mr. Banjo.
"Oh, dear. Is that the Captain's cake in your wagon?"
he asked. "I can take it from here if you'd like."

"Thank you," Ella said, "but I would really like to
finish what I've started."

When at last, she saw the lighthouse, she sped
up, hoping she wasn't late.

The Captain came to the door and spoke in a deep, gruff voice: "Are you the new delivery man?"

"No," Ella giggled.

"Well, isn't that an awfully big load for such a little girl?" He winked.

"Not too big," Ella assured him.

"Well, then," Captain Kernel laughed. "You must be bigger than you look!"

Ella returned home to the scent of cinnamon rolls baking.
"How did it go?" her mother asked.
"Fine," Ella replied.

"That was a very helpful idea," said her mother. "And while you were gone, I had an idea too."
"You did?" asked Ella, as she reached for the broom.

"Yes! I thought that later you could help me bake a Zanzibar Cake."

"Really?" asked Ella. Zanzibar Cake was her absolute favorite.

"Yes!" her mother smiled and handed Ella an apron. "I know it's too big." She paused. "But you'll grow into it before we know it."

She hoped her mother was right, because more than anything else . . .

Ella loved to help.